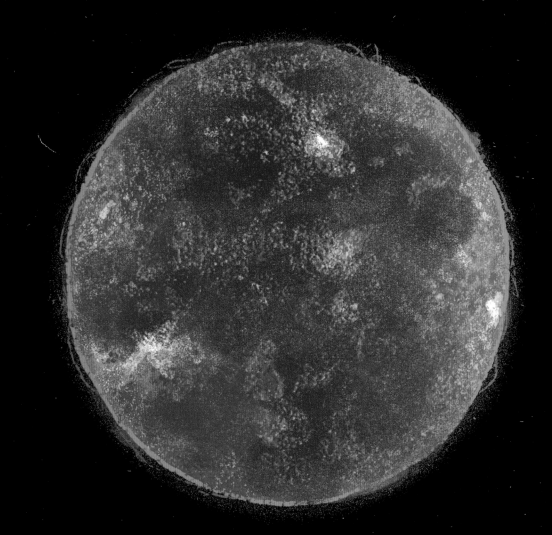

RED SUPERGIANT

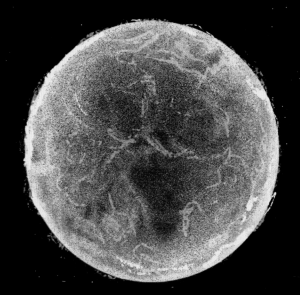

BLUE GIANT

To my son Mars, an on-point critique partner,
a late-night conversationalist, and a thief of my heart.
This idea began with you.
—L. L.


To my siblings, Jason, Jin, Jean, Tony, and Mike.
—J. T. K.

First published in 2019 by Page Street Kids,
an imprint of
Page Street Publishing Co.,
27 Congress Street, Suite 105, Salem, MA 01970
www.pagestreetpublishing.com

19 20 21 22 23 CCO 5 4 3 2 1

ISBN-13: 978-1-62414-693-0
ISBN-10: 1-624-14693-7

CIP data for this book is available from the Library of Congress.

This book was typeset in Publica Sans.
The illustrations were done digitally.
Printed and bound in Shenzhen, Guangdong, China.

Page Street Publishing uses only materials from suppliers who are
committed to responsible and sustainable forest management.

Page Street Publishing protects our planet by donating to nonprofits like The Trustees,
which focuses on local land conservation.

trustees

# NOVA

## THE STAR EATER

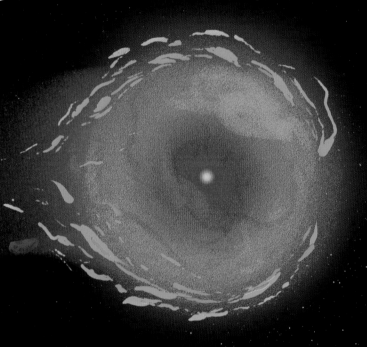

LINDSAY LESLIE

ILLUSTRATED BY JOHN TAESOO KIM

PAGE STREET KIDS

**Nova can't stop eating.** A munch here. A gobble there. A crunch, crunch, crunch.

She glides through the galaxy slurping up stars at the speed of light, never stopping to think whose stars they might be. Her favorites? Red supergiants. Yummy and plump. But she will eat any star she sees— white dwarfs, blue giants, binaries, whatever.

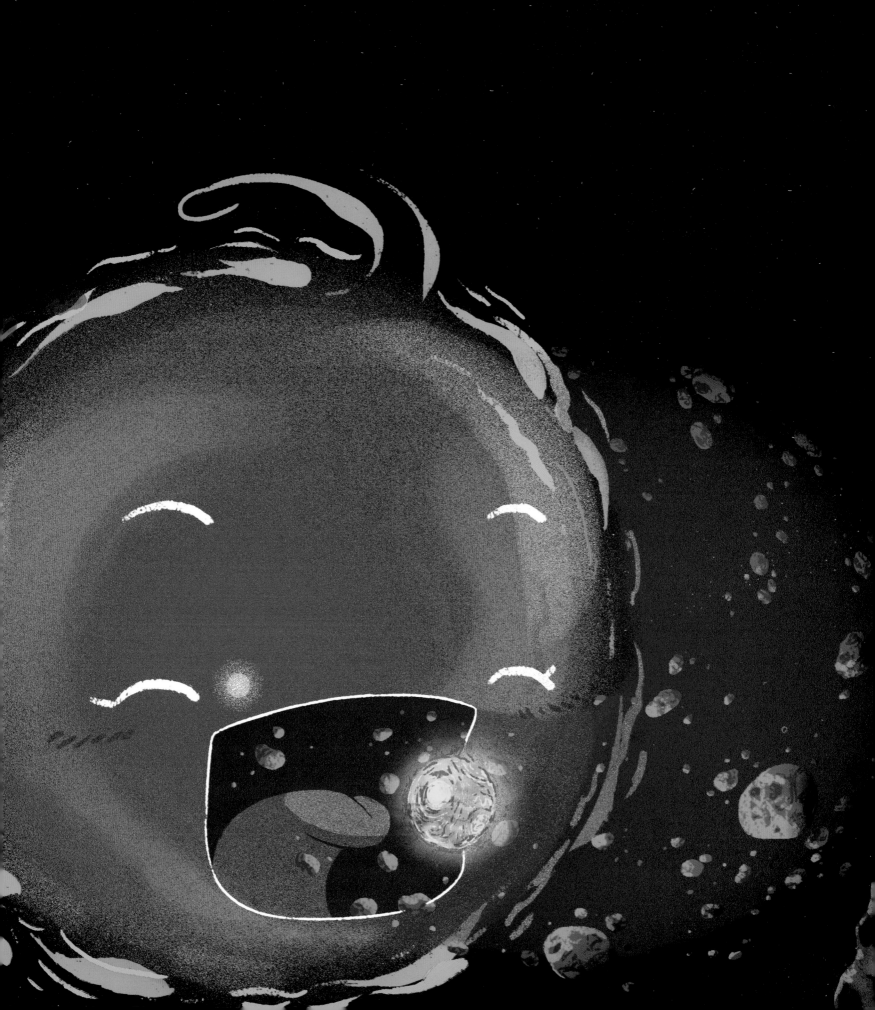

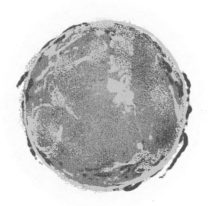

**One day,** she spots a juicy yellow dwarf near a pretty bluish-green planet. A planet wrapped in swirls like comet tails.

Nova sets her sights, opens wide, and . . .

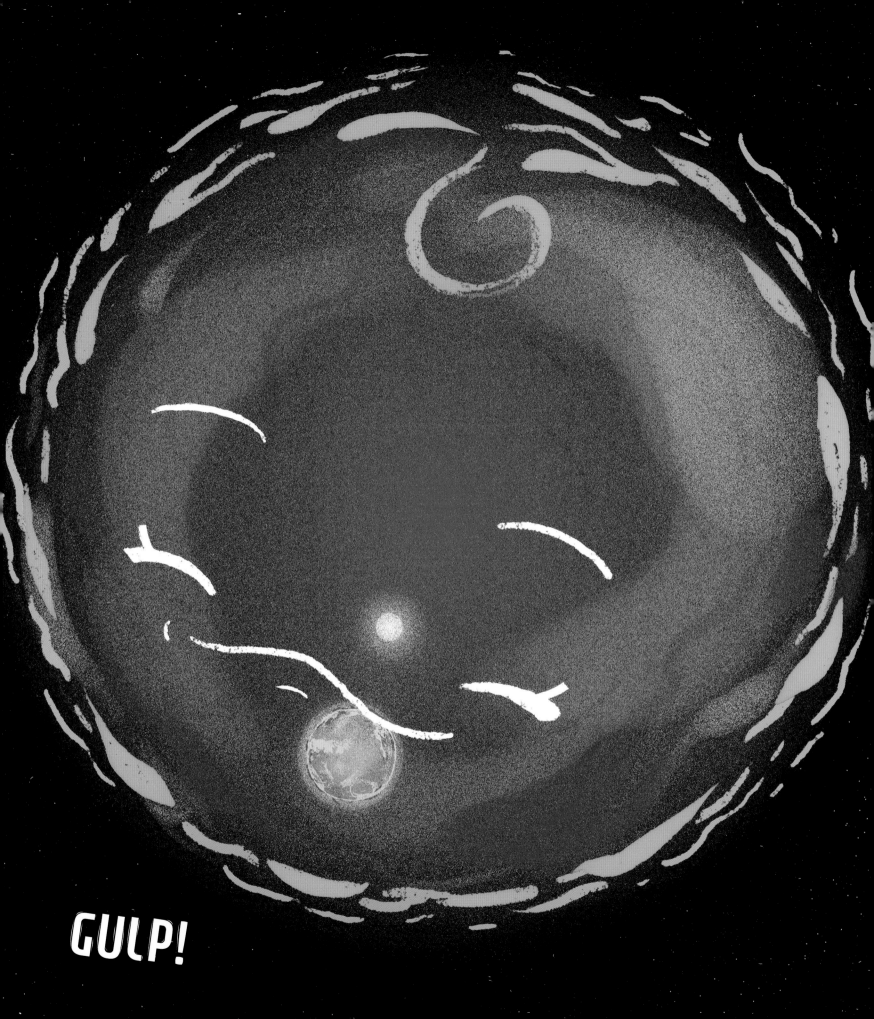

Little does Nova know,

her wild star-swallowing ways

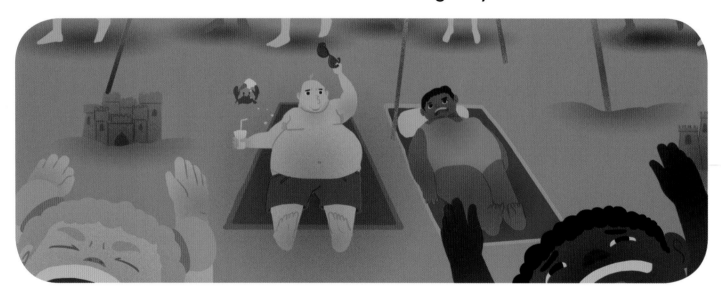

create panic on Earth.

Leaders from around the world gather and leap into action.
"There's no time to spare!" declares the leader from Egypt.
"Contact the space station!" commands the leader from France.
"Send our best astronauts!" instructs the leader from Brazil.

Satisfied after her cosmic treat, Nova bumps, bounces, and burps her way through the solar system.

Suddenly, she hears, "ATTENTION!"

"YIIIIIIIIKES! You surprised the stardust out of me!" Nova booms.

"We're representatives of Earth. What did you do to our Sun? We need it back . . . NOW!" cry the astronauts.

"Well, aren't you rude?" Nova fumes.

"Our apologies, but the situation is dire!" the astronauts yell. "The Sun is our star!"

"Your star? Well . . . I, uh . . . ate it."

# BURP!

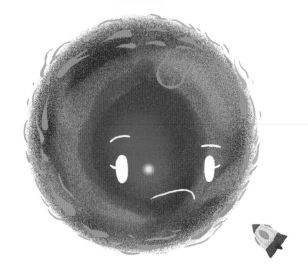

"But it's ours, and we need it!" they shout. "Please!"

"I needed it too, and it was *delicious*," Nova gushes. "What good is it to you?"

"What *good* is it? Are you serious?"

"Sirius? You mean 'the Dog Star'? No, no, no . . . I'm not a star. I'm Nova, the Star *Eater*," she boasts.

"Star eater? The Sun isn't a snack. The Sun gives us life!" they scream.

"Same here. But how does it give you life? You are much too small to eat a yellow dwarf."

"We don't *eat* it. The people on Earth need it to survive! The Sun provides energy for plants to grow, light so we can see, and heat to keep us warm. Without it, we'll freeze!"

"Earth? Is that the pretty bluish-green planet over there?"

"Yes! And those blues and greens will fade away without the Sun.

We'll lose track of the days. We won't have any seasons."

"Okay, okay! But what do you want me to do?" Nova burbles.
"Like I said, I ate it."

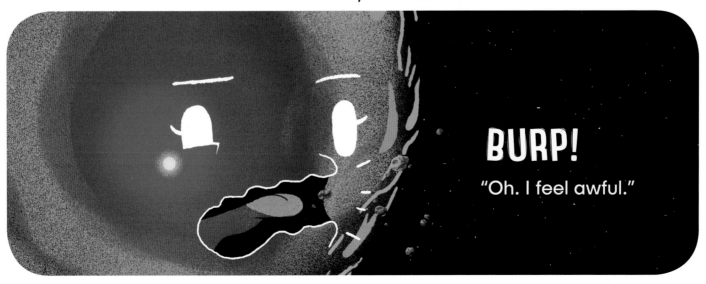

BURP!

"Oh. I feel awful."

*"Luminos* to Earth. *Luminos* to Earth. Any ideas on how to remove the Sun from Nova?"

The question is greeted with silence, until the leader from China asks, "Should we wait until it passes?"

"And risk the Sun being digested? Dangerous idea. But the Sun *is* magnetic. Maybe we can finally put our gigantic magnets to use," suggests the leader from India.

"No way! That could throw our entire solar sytem out of whack. Do we know of any stomach doctors with astronomical experience?" wonders the leader from Canada.

The room explodes with nervous chatter and debate.

"Ahem . . . 'scuse me . . . 'scuse me.

May I have your attention, please?"

All the faces, including her mom's, turn toward the girl.
"I know what we can do," she announces. "We could tickle her."

"Tickle her?" asks her mom, the leader from the United States.

"Yes, tickle her," says the little girl. "Make her laugh so hard she
 hiccups out our Sun."

"Best idea so far," admits the leader from Mexico.

"It just might work!" agrees the leader
 from Australia.

"How do you tickle a star eater?"
 inquires the leader from Ethiopia.

The room falls silent again as they
search for an answer.

"I think I know!" says the little girl.

"Nova, we've got a plan," say the astronauts. "Actually, a little girl came up with the idea. She wants to know if we could tickle you."

"Tickle me? Well, okay. I hope that's as fun as eating a red supergiant."

BURP.

"We've got to hurry," they say. "Follow us!"

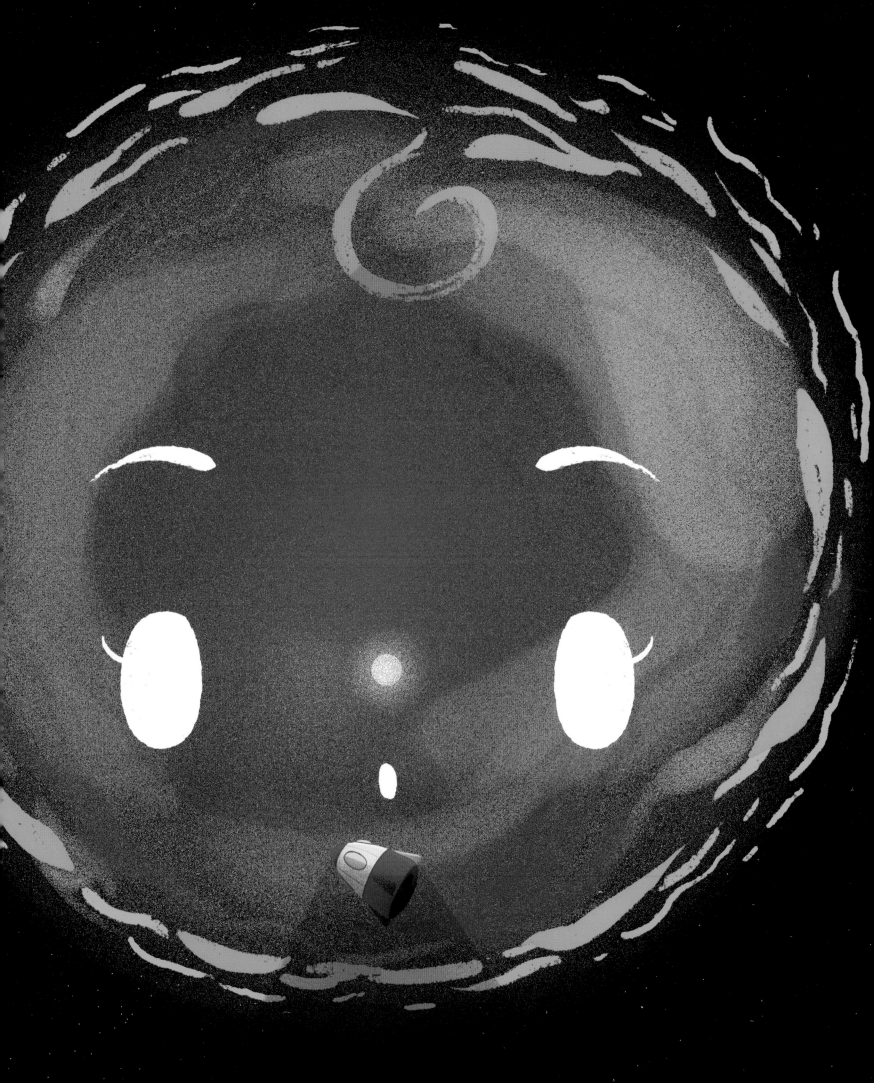

When she reaches Earth, Nova squirms and squiggles as the wind twirls below her.

**HA-HA-HA!**

**HEE-HEE!** She whirls and wiggles as the treetops tickle her back.

She jerks and jiggles as the ocean waves swish at her tummy. **HO-HO!**

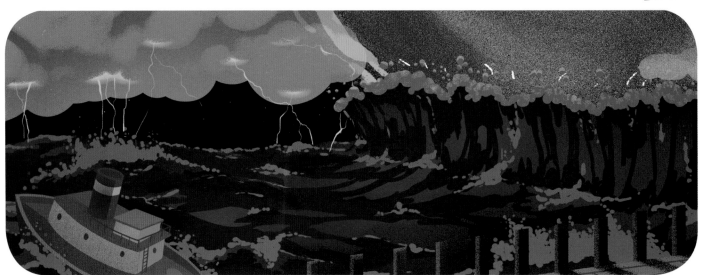

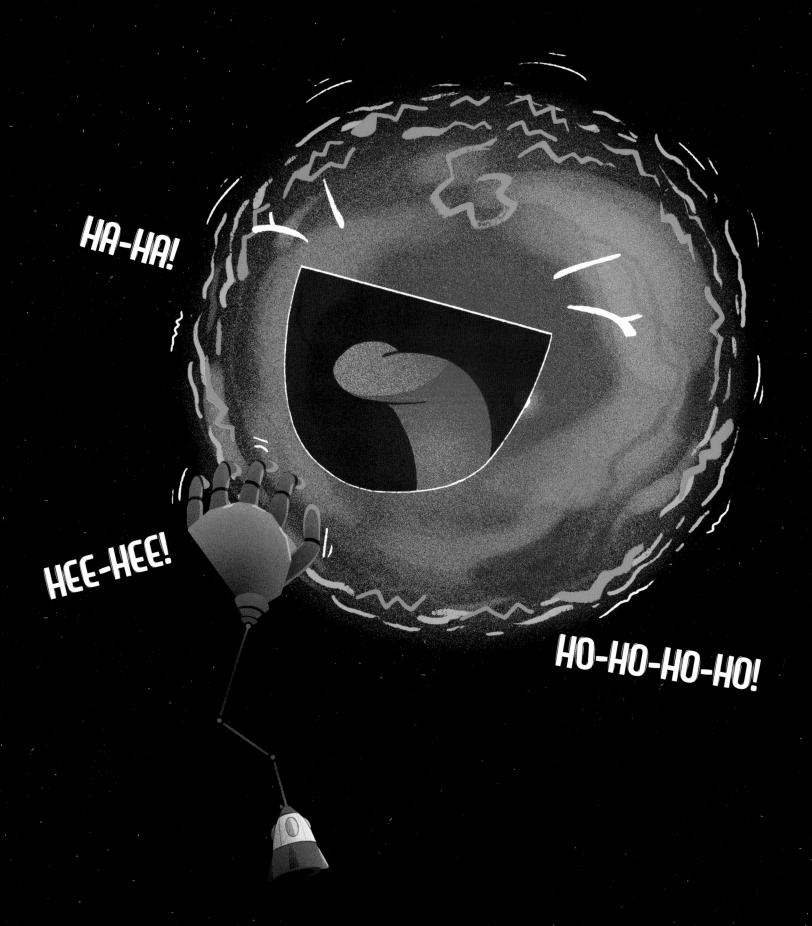

Then *Luminos* moves in, extends its robotic arms, and . . .
"Commence final phase of tickling," commands the little girl.

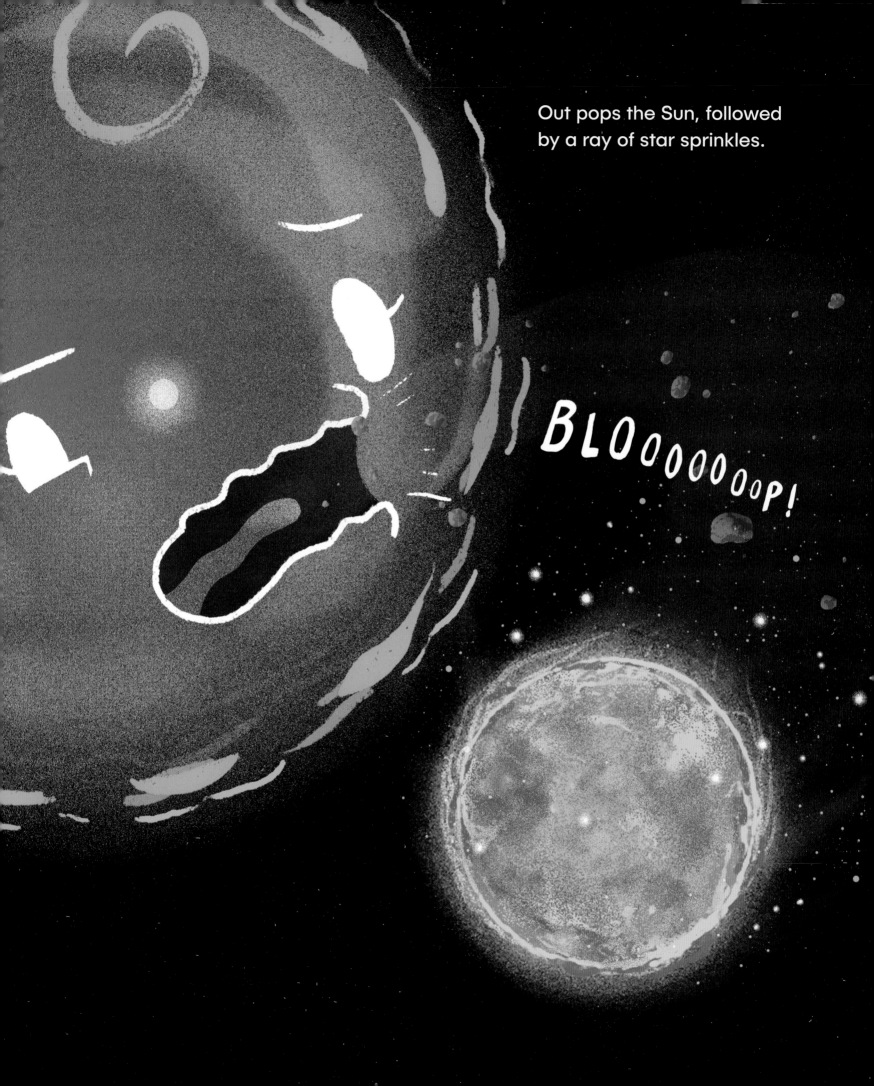

Out pops the Sun, followed by a ray of star sprinkles.

"Oooo, that felt silly! And you did me a favor. With all that gas, I think your tasty Sun had given me a case of the solar flares," says Nova. **HICCUP.**

Then she nudges the Sun back into place. "There. Right where I found it."

"Thanks, Nova. Next time, may we suggest eating a star near Orion's Belt? There are some to spare," say the astronauts.

And as Nova streaks through the universe looking for more stars to crunch, crunch, crunch, she often remembers the pretty bluish-green planet before snarfing.

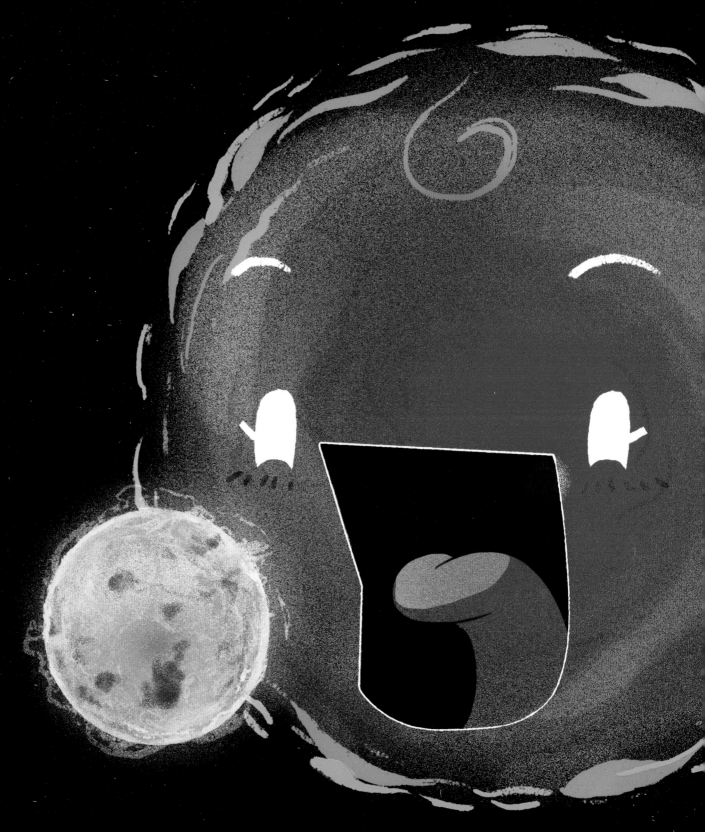

"Pardon me, is this your star?" she asks.

"Nurz, zeets nehs."

"Fantastic!" Nova exclaims.

GULP.

# EARTH'S SUN IS A STAR, NOT A SNACK

While the character Nova exists only in the imagination (and this book!), what the astronauts in the story say about the Sun is true. Earth revolves around the Sun—a star and the largest source of energy for the planet. This 4.5-billion-year-old yellow dwarf heats and lights the Earth, which helps plants grow. Humans and other living creatures depend on plants for oxygen and eat them for their nutrients . . . or at least they should (fruits and veggies rule!). But plants aren't the only ones to benefit directly from the Sun. The human body uses the Sun's rays to create vitamin D, which is essential for strong bones.

Beyond being an energy source, the Sun is the heart of its solar system. Without the Sun, Earth wouldn't have its diverse neighbors, including Mercury, Venus, Mars, Jupiter, Saturn, Uranus, and Neptune. The Sun's gravitational pull keeps all of Earth's large planetary friends, and even the tiniest of space debris, orbiting around it.

Speaking of orbits, Earth and the Sun are in a constant space dance. Earth spins on an axis, which creates days and nights. And it also revolves around the Sun, which creates the seasons as a result of Earth's tilt.

The Sun affects Earth in so many ways—from climate changes and the ocean currents to the weather and more. It is essential to Earth, so please, PLEASE, don't eat it!

## SELECTED BIBLIOGRAPHY

Merriam-Webster.com. Accessed September 2017. http://www.merriam-webster.com.

"Sun, Our Star." *NASA Science Solar System Exploration*, NASA's Science Mission Directorate. Accessed September 2017. https://solarsystem.nasa.gov/solar-system/sun/overview/.

Many thanks to Dr. Keely Finkelstein, of the University of Texas at Austin, for her astronomical expertise.

# GLOSSARY

**BINARY STARS:** two stars that revolve around each other

**BLUE GIANT:** a hot, massive, bright star getting toward the end of its lifetime; smaller than a red supergiant in size

**COMET:** a large chunk of rock, ice, and dust that often develops one or more long tails when it orbits near the Sun

**NOVA:** a star that suddenly increases in brightness and then fades away in a few months or years

**ORION'S BELT:** part of the Orion constellation, which consists of three stars—Alnitak, Alnilam, and Mintaka

**PLANET:** any large body that revolves around a star

**RED SUPERGIANT:** the largest type of star in terms of size in the universe

**SIRIUS:** the brightest star seen from Earth; also known as the Dog Star because it is part of the Canis Major ("the greater dog") constellation

**SOLAR FLARE:** a sudden outburst of energy from the Sun's surface

**SOLAR SYSTEM:** a sun and the planets that revolve around it

**STAR:** a ball-shaped body of gas that shines by its own light (like the Sun)

**WHITE DWARF:** a small, very dense star that is typically the size of a planet; what the Sun will become at the end of its "normal" lifetime

**YELLOW DWARF:** a medium-sized star, like the Sun

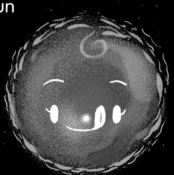